18978
KT-493-934

Falling Awake

by

Viv French

Illustrated by Roy Petrie

In memory of Clare

First published in Great Britain by Barrington Stoke Ltd
10 Belford Terrace, Edinburgh EH4 3DQ
Copyright © 2000 Viv French
Illustrations © Roy Petrie
The moral right of the author has been asserted in
accordance with the Copyright, Designs and
Patents Act 1988
ISBN 1-902260-54-6
Printed by Polestar AUP Aberdeen Ltd

The publisher gratefully acknowledges general subsidy
from the Scottish Arts Council towards the Barrington Stoke
teenage fiction series

A Note from the Author

I feel very strongly about drugs. I have to. I know – and love – a little boy whose Mum died from drugs just before his fifth birthday. He's a fantastic kid and his Mum was a great Mum. Her name was Clare.

She didn't take an overdose. She thought she was a 'responsible' drug user. She only took a little. But it was bad stuff and it killed her.

How do you tell a four-year-old that he's never going to see his Mum again?

This story is in memory of Clare.

Contents

GRACEMOUNT HIGH SCHOOL LIBRARY 18978

PERELLI

SPIKE

BULLET

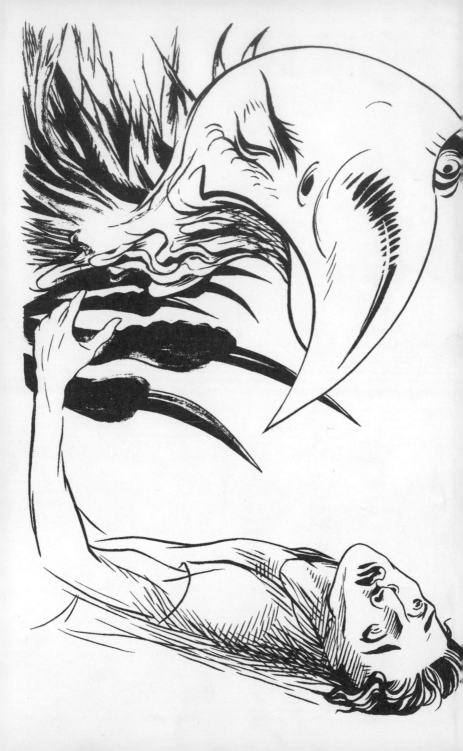

Chapter 1
Vulture

I was lying on the ground. It was hard and cold. I'd been asleep but I didn't know for how long.

I couldn't remember where I was. My head hurt. My eyes felt as if they were glued shut. I groaned, opened my eyes and saw a bird. A huge bird. A vulture.

I shut my eyes. I was dreaming. I *knew* I was dreaming. Vultures live in deserts, don't they? There was no way a real live vulture could be standing in front of me.

And vultures are birds. They fly about. A vulture wouldn't stand and stare at a 15-year-old boy with a thumping headache.

It had to be a dream. A bad dream.

I opened my eyes again. The vulture was still there. And he was still staring at me with his little beady eyes.

"Hello," he said, and winked.

This time I didn't shut my eyes. I stared back. It must be a trick, I thought. Someone was playing a game with me. And I didn't like games. I was Danny Perelli and Danny Perelli didn't play games.

I sat up and clutched my head. It hurt a lot.

"Got a headache?" The vulture shuffled nearer. His voice was posh like one of those newsreaders on TV.

I didn't take any notice. I wasn't in the mood for a chat – most of all when someone was trying to make me look an idiot.

I staggered to my feet, looking all around to see who was there.

No one. The alley was empty. High brick walls on either side and no sign of any human life.

In fact, now I came to look properly, there was no sign of anything. I couldn't see any houses, any trees, any telephone wires – and it was quiet. Very quiet indeed. So quiet that when the vulture shifted from foot to foot I could hear his claws scratching on the path.

"It's Danny Perelli, isn't it? Danny Perelli, number one cool kid." The vulture made a strange noise. It could have been a chuckle – if vultures chuckle, that is.

I turned and inspected the bird. He was dead scruffy. His head was bald, and his neck was bare wrinkly pink saggy flesh. His feathers were grey and dirty. He was fat.

"OK," I glanced behind me. Was I on my own? Yeah. Bullet Brown wasn't there. I was pretty certain that Bullet would never ever talk to a scabby fat bird with a bald head. Bullet would think that anyone who talked to a vulture was nuts.

Did I mind what Bullet thought? No way. Of course I didn't.

All the same, I wasn't going to give him the chance to have a go at me.

"OK," I said again. "What's going on?"

The vulture gave a small cough and dipped his head. "The name's Clark. How do you do?" He was so stupidly pleased with himself it made me laugh.

"*Clark?*" I said. "What sort of name is that?"

Clark fluffed his feathers. "No need to be rude," he said. "And just you remember, down here *I'm* the boss. Not you. Or Bullet Brown. By the way, which of you *is* top dog? I'd love to know."

I leaned against the wall and stared coldly at the bird. I reckoned I looked pretty cool on the outside – but my head was thumping like a pile driver.

All kinds of things were rushing through my mind. Was I really awake – or was this some kind of horrible dream? Was I going crazy? What exactly *was* Clark? What did he know about me and Bullet? How did he know it?

I stuck to the main point. He was annoying me. I didn't like being annoyed.

"Shut it," I said.

Clark began to hop up and down. "You don't know where you are, do you? That's not cool. And you don't know how you got here? That's not very cool either. You don't know *anything*, cool kid Danny Perelli!"

He was getting to me. I've never liked people telling me I don't know things.

I swung my boot at the bird. I felt a lot better when I heard him squawk. "Go and stuff yourself," I said, and I began walking away down the alley.

Chapter 2
Bullet Brown

I walked on and on down that alley, but it felt as if I was getting nowhere. It was all the same. High walls on either side, and nothing to see. Just the same dead grey sky above me. And it was quiet. No, it was more than quiet. There was no noise at all. Nothing. When I stopped all I could hear was my own breathing.

I went on and on. I had to – there was nothing else to do. I wasn't going to go back. I wasn't going to have a stupid scraggy bird getting at me. Although the more I thought about it, the more I thought it was a trick. And I could guess whose idea it was. Bullet's.

Ever since Bullet moved into our patch he'd been trying to be number one. He thought he was the only one with ideas. He thought he was the only one who knew what to do and where to go. And he wanted me and my mate Spike to trail along behind him – but I knew what he was up to.

Bullet was older than me and Spike – and bigger – but we'd been on our patch longer. Much longer.

Yeah. It was just like Bullet to work out a dumb trick with a stinking old vulture.

Well – it hadn't worked. He'd gone too far this time. As soon as I saw him again I'd sort him out. Or maybe me and Spike would sort him out between us.

Spike would do anything for me. Spike's been hanging out with me for years. Spike's OK.

The alley went on. And on. I began to wonder if I should have gone the other way.

Where was I, anyway? It wasn't the first time I'd woken up somewhere and not known where I was but usually I found out pretty damn quick.

I knew my town inside out. In fact, I knew it better inside than outside – if you know what I mean.

Spike and I knew it all. We knew the shelter under the bridge – a little tunnel that smelled of piss. We knew the dead end behind the car park where needles scrunched under your feet. We knew the secret places in the park where boys dragged giggling girls when it was dark. We knew all those places and we knew a whole lot more besides.

What did we do? Well – we drank a bit when we had the cash. When we didn't, we watched. We hid in trees or under the arch of the bridge or behind the car park wall and watched what the kiddie babes were doing.

Who were the kiddie babes? You know – the 13 and 14 year olds who think they're so clever.

The kiddies who think they're the first ever to have found out about sex and booze and the rest. We watched them snogging and rolling around in the grass. They thought they were drunk after half a can of cider. They were a joke.

But when Bullet came along that all changed.

When Bullet first moved in we thought he was all right. Spike and me, we kind of took him on. Showed him round, that sort of thing.

Then he began to show off. That was when he started telling us what to do and where to go. We tried freezing him out, but we couldn't shake him off. He was always there.

In the end, we didn't do much about it. He took it for granted that he was with Spike and me and we didn't argue. It was easier that way and sometimes it was OK.

I stopped walking. Thinking about Bullet was doing odd things to my brain.

I shook my head to clear it out. Boy! I wished I hadn't. A red hot stab of pain hit me between the eyes, and I gasped. It hurt – worse than any hangover I'd ever had.

I couldn't think straight.

For a second or two I thought I was under the bridge. I could even smell the sour old pee mixed with wet grass – and it was dark.

But I wasn't under the bridge. I was stuck in some alleyway, and somewhere behind me there was a foul old vulture squawking about.

Did it make sense? Of course it didn't. My head had settled back to a dull ache. I went on walking but Bullet was still hanging around in my mind.

Chapter 3
Easy Money

It was when Bullet came with us to watch the kiddie babes that he had this idea for making money.

Bullet loved money. He always seemed to have stashes of it, but he always wanted more. He thought me and Spike were daft because we never had any, so he dreamt up this scam for us.

We weren't that keen to begin with, but we weren't going to say no to easy money, were we? And we were fed up with Bullet calling us chicken. We'd show him we could be just as hard as he was.

And no. It wasn't dealing drugs, or anything like that. Well, not exactly. We were dealing aspirin. Yeah – that's right. Aspirin. Don't laugh. No one knew it was aspirin except Bullet and Spike and me. This was how Bullet planned it out.

I was the one who got hold of the aspirin. Dad always had loads of it, so I just nicked it when we needed new supplies. Spike was the one who sold it to the kiddies.

Bullet told him to tell them it was "*Great gear – the best!*"

Bullet said that Spike was so thick no one would ever think he was putting one over. That wasn't fair. Spike may be a few sandwiches short of a picnic, but he's not daft. Bullet was right about one thing, though. The plan worked.

We were careful, mind. We didn't do it all the time. And we always sold to the youngest kiddie babes. Bullet said the older ones would guess what we were up to. We were very careful.

Bullet and I watched when Spike met up with Jason, or Joe, or Rosie. It made Bullet laugh like a drain. The kiddie babes were so serious about it.

19

Sometimes I wondered if Spike knew that the little white pills were only aspirin. The way he talked you'd think he had the best gear going. "You'll have a great time now, Joe. Trust me, mate. And only a fiver each."

And Joe would say, "Good stuff, Spike. Here you are. Yeah. Thanks, mate."

I have to admit that those fivers came in very handy. Spike and Bullet and me – we were never short of cash. Bullet never seemed to spend his, but Spike and I had a good time. We splashed it around and it was great.

I was jingling coins in my pockets as I walked down that long, long alley. I could feel a couple of notes too. I pulled them out to check them over, and saw that there were five of them. Five £20 notes.

One hundred quid. *One hundred quid.*

Weird.

I couldn't remember where it had come from. I could see the five £20 notes in between my fingers, but I couldn't remember anything about them. When I tried to pin down a thought, or a memory, my mind went dead. Just like a computer crash. Blank. Nothing, and I felt stranger and stranger the more I tried to boot my brain back into gear.

I shook my head (ouch, and a bad ouch at that) and went on walking. I walked faster and faster. I wasn't feeling good. I needed to get out. I needed to go home.

Hang on a moment.

I stopped.

The brick walls on either side of me were higher. And was the alley getting narrower?

I turned round to check behind me and there *he* was. The vulture. Clark. Uglier than ever. *And* bigger. I'd swear he was twice the size he was when I first saw him. And now he was grinning. *Grinning!*

"Hello," he said. And he winked. Again.

That did it. I didn't know where I was.

I didn't know where I was going. I was feeling grotty and I had a little weird white blank in my head about that hundred quid.

Maybe that was worrying me more than I wanted to admit – even to myself. The whole thing was like the worst sort of nightmare and now a tricksy scabby vulture was winking at me. I lost it.

I yelled, I screeched and I grabbed that bird by his scabby, scaly feet. I swung him up and I swung him round – and then I slung him as high as I could. Over he went, over the wall. Boy, did he squawk!

"*Great*," I told myself. "Good going, Danny Perelli. And now to get out of this place."

I began running back the way I'd come. I wasn't getting anywhere going the other way. So sure as hell I would going this way. And there wouldn't be any dumb bald birds squawking at me, either. So I ran ... and I ran ... and I ran.

I ran until my heart was pounding louder than my head. My legs began to feel like lead, but I forced myself on faster and still faster.

Then I stopped.

I was puffing so hard I thought my lungs would burst. My head was throbbing. I was back at the place where I'd woken up. I knew it was the place, because there was my baseball cap, screwed up against the wall. And I could see something else, too.

Clark was standing in the middle of the alleyway. He was just as scruffy as he was when I first saw him. No better, no worse. His feathers were grey and dirty, exactly the way they were before.

But he was bigger. Much bigger. He was nearly half my height, and he was chuckling again.

"Hello," he said.

Chapter 4
Hearing Voices

I stared at Clark and he stared back at me. I wanted to make a dash past him and run on down the alley, but I didn't. There was an odd look in his eye, even though he was still chuckling. He looked mean. It suddenly struck me that he had nasty looking claws. And a sharp beak. I found

myself thinking that vultures eat meat.
Dead meat.

"Well," I said. "Fancy seeing you again."

Clark didn't answer. He took a step
towards me. I stepped back. It makes sense
to be careful when a bird is three times life
size and armed with claws and a big, sharp
beak. I sized up the gap between him and
the walls. It wasn't big.

I tried the oldest trick in the book. I
pointed behind him, "*Watch out!!!*" I yelled.

It worked. Clark jumped as if he'd been
shot and spun round. I ran ... and I was past
him.

I legged it away down the alley. Danny Perelli had won again! I was grinning as I hurtled round a corner. I was the best at getaways. Spike was too. I could remember *loads* of times when we'd left a posse of kids standing with their mouths wide open and their eyes popping, all ready to be shrieked at by Sir at school, or the law or whoever. Suckers.

Once I was round the corner, I slowed down a bit. The alley was getting wider. I was certain I was going the right way. It wasn't so deadly quiet, either. I could hear voices. It sounded like they were coming towards me. *Great!* I'd soon be out and back on my own patch. I slowed down to a fast walk, and pushed my hands into my pockets.

The hundred quid. I'd forgotten about it. I began to pull the notes out. Then I shoved them back, right down to the bottom of my pocket under my gum and stuff. Just touching the money made me feel strange.

My head was full of empty space and I suddenly felt sick. It made me think of one of the times when Spike and I were starving. We slipped off down the corner shop, and helped ourselves to a couple of meat pies from the bins at the back. Spike said there couldn't be anything wrong with them because they were still wrapped up in that plastic stuff. Besides, we were so hungry we'd have eaten anything.

We holed up under the bridge and ate the pies. That night we were so ill we thought we were going to die, but we didn't. We threw up for hours and hours and hours.

The feeling I had then just before I started heaving my guts up was exactly the same as the feeling I got when I touched that money. Out of it. Floaty. Weird. And I still had no idea where the money had come from.

Action. That was what I needed. Action. If you do something – anything – it means you don't have to think. I'd learnt that when I was tiny. Oh, not the sort of thinking when you have to decide where you're going and what you're going to do when you get there. The other sort of thinking. You know. About things that have happened to you. The sort of thinking that

slithers into your brain in the dark of the
night, and makes you think stupid stuff like
what if Mum hadn't walked out? And what
would she think if she could see me now?
And what would she think about Bullet?
Yucky stuff.

But I knew what to do. I'd got it sussed.
No problem! Action. That was what I
needed.

I began to swing my arms as I walked. It
didn't take me long to feel better. The path
was getting wider and the voices were
getting nearer.

I began to make plans. I'd stop whoever
was coming and check out where I was.
Then I'd know the way back. I'd grab
something to eat – if there was anything,

that is – and then I'd go down to the park and see what was going on. Spike would be there, for sure. We always met up in the park on a Saturday.

My mind skidded and flipped over. I don't know any other way to describe it. It was like those dreams when you're walking and you suddenly drop down a huge step you never knew was there.

I didn't know if it was Saturday. I didn't know what day it was.

I didn't know. I really didn't. I didn't have a clue. It could have been any day of the week. And the more I tried to remember, the more I couldn't remember.

The last thing that was clear in my head

was walking across the park to meet Bullet. I was dropping off some more aspirin. I'd found a full bottle of the stuff beside Dad's bed. It didn't have a label on it, but I had a quick squint inside and it seemed fine.

I could remember sitting on a swing and talking to Bullet and Spike. They laughed at me because I kept blowing my nose. I'd got a bit of a cold. Spike said I looked rough, and Bullet told him he was a lovely Mummy – but after that?

Nothing. Zilch.

I couldn't remember anything more. And when I tried to think if it was yesterday when I was in the park, or even the day before – *whoops!* My mind flipped again. My heart started racing inside me as if I'd been dashing for the bus and a voice inside my head began to whisper, "Crazy. You're going crazy, Danny Perelli."

No. I shook my head. It was stupid. I'd remember soon. It was just a blip. Maybe a bug. Yeah – of course! That's what it was. I was ill. You see weird things when you're ill, right? Like when I ate those meat pies.

I shook my head again. I needed to see a real human being. I could just imagine Spike saying, "Hey, Danny – what's up, man? You look terrible!"

I could still hear the voices. I began to run again. I needed to get to those voices, and I needed to get there fast. I swerved round another corner – and there they were. A bunch of kiddie babes – Rosie and Joe and Jason and Lisa.

The kiddies came hurrying towards me, and they were making one hell of a noise. I couldn't hear what they were saying, but they weren't messing about. They looked angry. Really angry. Joe was shaking his fist and yelling, and Lisa was shouting too.

It was really hard not to rush up to them. I had to swallow hard, and bang my arm against the wall. I mean, who was I? A little kid lost in the park? Danny Perelli, running for help? No way. Not smart. Not smart at all. I slowed down to my usual swagger.

"Hi," I said. "You here too?"

They didn't answer. They didn't even look up. They blanked me. It was as if I wasn't there. As if I was invisible. The cheek! I moved to block their way.

"Oi! You lot! I'm talking to you! You deaf, or what?"

That's when it happened. They walked straight through me. Straight through, and out the other side.

Chapter 5
Panic

I can't tell you what it felt like when they walked through me. I don't know. It didn't hurt. It was like fog, or mist, or smoke. Only it wasn't the kiddies that were the fog. It was me. How can I explain it? Look at your arm. Wave it about. Now pinch it. Real? Of course it is. But I wasn't real. Not to those four kids.

I couldn't believe them. I ran after them. "*Oi! Rosie! Jason! Look – it's me!*"

I tried to grab them. I couldn't. My hand went into the mist, and after the third or fourth time I couldn't try again. It was like the very worst nightmare I'd ever had.

I yelled. I shouted until I was hoarse. Not one of them even glanced back. Seconds later they were gone.

I pinched my arm until my eyes watered. It felt real enough. I kicked the wall. That hurt even more. I stamped my feet and I could hear the thud! thud! thud! All the time that little whispering voice in my head was getting louder and louder.

"Crazy? You're not just crazy. You're mad, mad, mad, mad – "

"*No! No! No!*" I was screeching, like my Mum did when my Dad thumped her, but I couldn't help it.

I threw myself onto the ground. The tarmac was cold and hard and real. It was beautiful. I shut my eyes and lay there for a minute. I was Danny Perelli, I told myself. I was ill, I wasn't mad. I was OK. I was fine. In a second or two I'd open my eyes and I'd be in the park. Or under the bridge. Or on the bathroom floor.

I opened my eyes and saw Clark.

He was big. He was *so* big. I could see his scaly yellow feet. His huge steely claws looked like they could rip open just about anything. When I looked up, all I could see was a swell of dirty feathers. From where I was lying it looked as if he was taller than the wall.

He bent his head down. He peered at me with first one shiny little eye and then the other. Then as he turned his head, I could see the sloppy wrinkly naked skin round his neck. It was disgusting.

I wanted to get up, to be on my feet. It was a horrible feeling, lying on my back and being stared at. I was against the wall and he was right in front of me. I couldn't roll away. I lay where I was and I sweated.

Why was I sweating? I was scared. I was so scared my insides were knotted into an agony of sheer terror. I'd beaten this bird up, hadn't I? I'd kicked him, chucked him around, tricked him. And here he was, back again – and he was *huge*.

I was so scared I thought I was going to wet myself.

"Hello," said Clark, and he took a step or two backwards.

I was shaking as I scrambled up. My legs were jelly. I had to lean against the wall. I tried to make it look as if I was just there for the view. What was the view? A six foot tall bald fat vulture. A six foot tall fat vulture who probably wanted to beat me senseless and tear me into shreds for his next meal.

Clark was nodding at me. "So you saw your friends. Angry, were they?"

I didn't know what to say, so I said nothing. If I'd thought my legs would hold me up, I'd have dashed after Jason and the others. Even if they couldn't see me at least I could see them. They were real people.

And who knows? Maybe they were only messing around before. Maybe I'd had another funny blip. Maybe I'd only imagined that they'd walked through me – but I couldn't quite make myself believe that. I was beginning to find it hard to believe anything.

"Didn't you wonder why they were so angry?" Clark said, and his shiny little eyes winked and winked at me. "Don't you want to know?"

I still didn't say anything. I wasn't taking in what Clark was saying. I was beginning to feel my legs again, and I was wondering if I could make a run for it. The trouble was, I didn't know which way to go. Besides, I was getting one message loud and clear. Wherever I went and whatever I did, Clark was going to be right behind me. Or in front. And getting bigger each time.

A picture flashed into my brain of a super-sized Clark about a mile high. I shivered. Part of my brain told me, "That's not possible." But then nothing that was happening to me was possible. I stayed where I was.

Clark shook his head. "Oh dear, I was so looking forward to telling you what they were saying." And he turned round and shambled away down the alley.

I didn't know what to do. My mind was whirling in circles of growing panic. What did it all mean? What was happening? I couldn't make any sense of it. I felt as if everything inside my head was about to burst out. Half of me wished it really would. Then the awfulness of it all would be over once and for all.

What was happening to me?

I wasn't real to the kiddie babes. I was – well, like a ghost. But I seemed to exist OK in Clark's world, but what sort of world was that? A world where walls got higher and higher and a giant vulture towered above me. A giant vulture who wanted to do what? The knots in my stomach grew tighter.

I watched Clark go. He was heading the way the kiddie babes had gone. I didn't know what to do so I trailed after him. It was pathetic. Believe you me, if I'd thought there was anywhere else to go, I'd have gone. If there was anything else to do, I'd have done it. But there wasn't.

As I dragged along behind Clark, I began to take in what he'd been saying. I began to take in what he'd said about the kiddies being so angry. Did it matter? I'd been so shocked that they hadn't seen me that nothing else had mattered at the time.

Why was Clark making such a mystery

of it? I began to hurry to catch him up, but before I reached him he turned round, exactly as if he'd read my mind.

"Oh yes," Clark said. "They were angry. *Very* angry. They found out they were being tricked, you see. They were feeling big and bold and daring because they were taking drugs. Then they found out they were being fooled. They weren't big and bold and daring at all. They were just silly little kiddie babes and they couldn't even tell anyone."

Clark began to chuckle. "What could they say? 'Oh Mummy – I thought I was taking drugs but I was being conned!'" He began to chuckle louder. "No. So they've got to get the guy that sold them the stuff and guess who that is?" And Clark began to chortle louder and louder.

My eyes bulged, and my throat went dry. "They – they've found out? About the aspirin?"

Clark was hopping from foot to foot and flapping his wings. "Oh yes, yes!!!" He saw my face, and stopped for a second or two. "Oh, Danny Perelli! What are you worrying about? They don't blame you. How can they? You're dead!" And off he went into another fit of laughing and cackling and flapping his wings.

Chapter 6
Talk ... Talk ... Talk

I was lying on the ground under the bridge. No, I wasn't. I was lying on the ground in a long, long alleyway with high brick walls, but I could smell old pee and wet grass. I could hear someone shouting. Yes, I could hear that. They were shouting very loudly. They were shouting, "*No! No! No! No!*"

And then I knew it was me. I was shouting. And I was in between those high brick walls and I was on my own. There was no vulture.

But now I could hear footsteps and I struggled up onto my knees and I prayed – yes, I did. I really prayed that it was something – someone – anything coming to help me.

It was Bullet. He came round the corner and he was whistling until he saw me. Yes – he really did see me. I looked at his eyes, and I could tell that he could see me. I crawled towards him, and I was crying.

"Bullet – get me out of here! Get me out!" I caught his arm – a solid, fleshy, chunky arm. It was wonderful to touch a real living human being – but Bullet knocked me away from him. His face was white and he was trembling all over.

"Get off me!" he yelled, and his voice was shaking. "Get off! You're dead – get off!"

I clutched at his leg and I hung on as hard as I could. He tried to kick me off. He hammered with his fists on my back, but I wouldn't give in. He began to swear at me, and then, as I hung on and on, he began to beg me to let go. I still clung on. He began trying to drag me, little by little, along the ground. As he heaved and pulled at me he began to talk, faster and faster.

"You asked for it, you know, you and Spike. You were such losers. It was so easy – like taking sweeties from a baby in a pram.

You didn't ever know, did you? All the time you were selling those teeny little aspirins to the teeny little kiddies, I was selling the big stuff to the big guys. I've been doing that for months. But the law began watching. I had to have a plan ... and I did.

"Oh, it was so easy. There you were, Spike and you, flashing money around all over the place. Where were losers like you and Spike going to get money like that? Even your granny would have guessed you were up to something! When the cops got too near to be comfortable, I decided to move out. But I thought I'd stir things up a bit before I went. Just in case they spotted that I wasn't around any more. But how?

"I told the kiddie babes you had conned them. All those fivers they'd handed over!

They weren't happy to hear they'd paid a fiver for just one *aspirin*.

"So they're out there – and they're looking for Spike. They'd be looking for you too, if you hadn't taken those pills."

Bullet slapped his hand on his pocket. I heard a rattling sound. "I should thank you for those. Dunno what's wrong with your Dad, but these are real. Highers. Trust you to get the real thing and not even notice. You should have heard yourself down there in the park.

"'Here you are, Bullet,' you said, 'here's some more aspirin. I was going to take one for my horrid little cold that's made my poor little nose all red, but I didn't. It's a new pack.'

55

"I stuffed some in your face and you thanked me. That's when I saw that they were the real thing. You never even made it past the bridge. Whack! Down you went. Then Spike was fussing over you. Well you must have swallowed four or five. Big mistake, Danny Perelli. One to get high, two for the sky, three and I'm flying and four? Death's door. By the way, I'm taking the rest of them with me. They'll come in useful."

Bullet stopped pulling me along, and suddenly bent down. "And one more thing. I put a little dosh in your pocket. When they pull your stone cold stinking little body out from under the bridge, they'll find that dosh. Then they'll know for certain you're the brains behind all this nasty drug dealing that's been going on. Now – *let me go, dead boy!*"

Bullet smashed my head against the brick wall so hard that stars burst into little green and gold sparkles all round the edges of my brain. As I faded away I saw Bullet's arms grow longer and feathery – grey, dirty feathers. His head was small and bald. A ruff of feathers grew below the sloppy wrinkly skin of his neck. His eyes were beady.

Chapter 7
Under The Bridge

I was lying on the ground, and it was hard and cold. I couldn't remember where I was. My head hurt. My eyes felt as if they had been glued shut. I groaned, opened my eyes and saw Spike. His face was a blur in the darkness under the bridge.

"Oh man," he said, "I thought you was dead, Danny."

I tried to shake my head, but it hurt too much. Much too much.

Spike began pulling at my arm. "Danny, mate, we've got to get out of here. The kiddie babes – they know what we've been doing. Bullet was shouting about it when he dragged you up here. You should have heard him, Danny. He was yelling at you, telling you how he was so clever, how you and me was losers. It was horrible, Danny. He kept yelling at you and dragging you along the ground and banging your head and then he called you 'dead boy' and he whacked your head on the bridge and ran off."

I gave a feeble groan.

It was all I could do.

Spike was still pulling at my arm, but he stopped when he heard me groaning.

"Oh, Danny, mate – don't blame me. I would have stopped him, honest I would – but I thought you'd had it. I thought you was past it. Honest, I did. When you fell over I thought you was so dead. You was grey, Danny – you was all grey – and your eyes was all rolled into the top of your head. I never seen anything like that before, Danny. It was horrible." And Spike scrubbed at his eyes with his fist as if he was trying to rub out what he'd seen.

I moaned again.

Spike suddenly froze. "There they are!

They're coming! Come on, Danny – come on!" Spike hauled on my arm as if he was drowning. "You've *got* to get up. Bullet blabbed. He told the kiddies it was all rubbish. He's told them we was tricking them all the time. They want blood, Danny – come on. I'll help you."

It wasn't any good. I tried to drag myself up onto my hands and knees, but I couldn't do it. Spike pulled and heaved, but I was like a sack of lead. And my head – my head was full of red hot knives twisting and twisting and twisting.

I could hear the noise now. I could hear the shouting – and it sounded exactly the way it had when I was in that alleyway. Somehow I didn't think they'd walk through me this time, though.

"You go," I croaked at Spike. "Go on. You go."

Spike finally let me drop back down. "No," he said. "We're mates, ain't we, Danny? And mates stick together." And he sat down beside me.

We didn't have to wait long. We could hear Rosie and Jason the clearest and they were yelling their heads off.

"*Spike! Spike!* Come on out and take what's coming to you!"

I looked at Spike. It was dark under the bridge, but I could see him looking back.

"They're after me, Danny," he said. "They think – they know you took them pills. They think it served you right and now they're after me. But if they find you here too ..."

Spike didn't finish what he was saying, but he didn't need to. I could hear the kiddie babes tearing their way through the bushes.

It was then that it happened. Something clicked in my brain and I started thinking. I'd been cheating. I'd been selling the kiddie babes rubbish. Maybe ... maybe I was rubbish too.

My head was spinning. What was the difference between me and Bullet? Nothing.

Bullet used me to cover up his dealing. I used the kiddies to get cash. We were as bad as each other.

But what about Spike? He'd never have thought of selling drugs by himself. He just did what I did. He just did what I told him to do. He always had ...

I took a deep breath and I heaved myself up onto my hands and knees. It hurt like hell but I made myself crawl out. Out towards the open air.

"Danny!!" Spike made a grab at my ankle. "Come back!" But he was too late. I was already face to face with the kiddie babes.

I didn't know I looked that bad. When they saw me they stopped so suddenly several of them staggered and fell over. It would have been funny if their faces hadn't been so terrified. They were pale and their eyes stood out on stalks. They were shivering and shaking. Jason clutched Rosie, and they stared and stared and stared at me. They didn't say a word. You'd have thought I was a ghost.

Then I understood. It was what they did think.

"No," I croaked. "It's me, Danny." I held out my hand, but it didn't help. They took a step or two backwards. They were totally silent.

I stared at them for a second. Then I had an idea and I dug my hand into my back pocket. There it was. The hundred quid. The dosh Bullet had stuffed there. I hauled it out and threw it at the kiddie babes.

"Here you are. Take it. I'm sorry. I'm really, really sorry. And it wasn't Spike – it was my idea. And I'll give you all your cash back, but leave Spike alone. He only did what I told him – "

"Shut up, Danny."

I jumped. It was Spike, but I'd never heard him sound like that.

"Shut up, Danny." He was walking past me, walking towards the kiddies. "It was me just as much as you. I knew what we was doing. 'Course I did. I ain't that dim. And I know aspirin is bad stuff – oh, not as bad as Es and all that – but it's bad if you take too much. Makes you bleed inside. I knew that, so I swapped it. I swapped it for those little sherbet things they sell at the sweetie shop. I chucked the aspirin down the bog. So I'm a cheat twice over. So – come and get me."

I stared at Spike, and so did the kiddie babes. Then I had another thought. Clunk. Just like that. They weren't kiddie babes. Not at all. They were just kids – blokes and girls, ordinary kids. Just a bit younger than me. A year ago I'd been the same.

Now they were muttering to each other. They were looking at me, and at Spike and then talking some more in whispers. Then Rosie stepped forward.

"We think you're sad, Danny Perelli. *So* sad. You're a real loser. We don't want your stinking money. We don't want you saying you're sorry. We used to think you were cool, we used to look up to you – but we were *so* stupid. You're nothing. Nothing at all. And if it's people like you who do drugs, then you can keep them. You're dirt. At least Spike was thinking about us – a bit. But don't worry about us beating you up any more. We wouldn't want to get our hands dirty."

Rosie walked away. All the other kids went with her and then I heard the wail of a police siren coming nearer and nearer and nearer. For a moment or two I thought the loud moaning shriek was coming from inside me. It was how I felt.

Chapter 8
The End

It was a long time before I got right again. They pumped out my stomach at the hospital, and they asked me questions over and over and over. In the end the police let me off with a severe warning. I was lucky. In a way. They got Bullet. The money he'd stuffed in my pocket was marked so it could be traced. The police had got onto him sooner than he'd guessed and they'd laid some kind of trap. He's doing time in a young offender's prison now.

I sometimes think I'd rather be inside. It's not a good life when everybody turns the other way when they see you coming.

Well, everyone except Spike. Good old Spike.

Spike says it'll be OK in the end. And he told me something else. Bullet's name wasn't really Bullet.

It was Clark.

Barrington Stoke would like to thank all its readers for commenting on the manuscript before publication and in particular:

Rosemary Bean
Kate Berry
Shaun Burns
Sarah Cubitt
Helen Foster
Judith Gauge
Laura Green
Clare Hodge
Antonia Jenkins
Lawrence Johnson
Jane-Ann Lawson
Fay Longdon

Anna Parker
Dorothy Porter
Douglas Richmond
Louise Roberts
Patrick Sessions
Jordan Souness
Darren Stacey
Moira Thomson
Luke Turnbull
Aimee Vinall
Greta Walker
Dionne Wonta

Become a Consultant!

Would you like to give us feedback on our titles before they are published? Contact us at the address or website below – we'd love to hear from you!

Barrington Stoke, 10 Belford Terrace, Edinburgh EH4 3DQ
Tel: 0131 315 4933 Fax: 0131 315 4934
E-mail: barringtonstoke@cs.com
Website: www.barringtonstoke.co.uk

More Titles

Playing Against the Odds
by Bernard Ashley

Chris's world is turned upside down by the arrival of Fiona in his class. His loyalties are torn in two as more and more thefts take place at school. But nothing can prepare Chris for the betrayal that lies ahead ...

To Be A Millionaire
by Yvonne Coppard

The news that a famous film director is in town sets Jack's mind racing. At last, he thinks, he's finally got his break! All he has to do is to be in the right place at the right time. This time it's up to him.

Runaway Teacher
by Pete Johnson

Scott thinks teachers are boring. Then a new teacher arrives - a teacher with very different ideas about lessons, rules and school. But when too many rules are broken, Scott learns just how complicated friendship and loyalty can be.

Alien Deeps
by Douglas Hill

When Tal plunges through the protecting field on the edge of the Clear Zone, he knows that he is leaving the only safe place on the planet. Beyond it lies the unknown, a world outside human control. But is the unknown the greatest danger in the alien deeps?

The Shadow on The Stairs
by Ann Halam

People say Joe's new house is haunted. Every night, he looks for the shadow on the attic stairs. Sometimes he thinks he can see it, sometimes he knows he can't. He tells himself that he isn't scared and wishes he could get the idea that it is evil out of his mind ...